THE AIRPLANE EFFECT

by Marc Gaskins,
Sasha Johnson,
Angelo Porter, and Sean Ross

Reach Education, Inc. | Washington, DC

Reach: Books by Teens
Published by
Reach Education, Inc.
www.reachincorporated.org

DEDICATION

This book is dedicated to all those who just
want to be a kid again.

Vincent lies in his
hospital bed
watching TV.

He is tired of watching commercials.

He throws down the remote control.

He looks out the window and sees kids playing.

"Mom, I wish I could go outside," Vincent says.

Vincent likes to play basketball.

He likes to fly kites.

He likes to lie down on the grass and watch the airplanes fly overhead.

But he can't do any of those things now.

Vincent gets so bored that he asks, "Mom, what can I do?"

"For right now, all you can do is watch TV," his mom replies.

She's sitting in a chair knitting, knitting, and knitting.

Vincent picks up his journal and starts to write.
He writes:

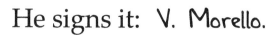

I have been going through chemo. I am losing my hair. I don't want to give up but it's hard. I just want to feel like a kid again and play outside.

He signs it: V. Morello.

Vincent hears an airplane preparing to land outside. It sounds like:

Whoooooooooooooooo.

He rips out his journal paper and folds it into an airplane.

As he is about to throw it his mother says, "You can't throw things in here."

Vincent sighs. His mother keeps knitting, knitting, and knitting.

That night, Vincent can't sleep because he is still upset about what his mother told him.

He sees his paper airplane lying on the table next to him.

He grabs it.

He throws the airplane up in the air.

It hits the ceiling fan and flies out the window.

Vincent jumps up out of bed and runs to the window. He looks up at the stars.

His plane flies like a bird piercing the moon.

Mesmerized by the night sky, he hopes someone will find his plane.

He feels at ease now so he can rest.

It's a very windy night.

The airplane travels and travels.

It goes through the city, passing the skyscrapers, the shopping centers, the restaurants, and the neighborhood playgrounds.

There's an open window on the 4th floor of a townhouse by the playground.

The airplane quietly makes its home inside the room.

The next morning, a little girl named Sally Pecan wakes up and finds the airplane on the floor in her room. She says, "Where did this come from?"

She opens it up. Inside is a message. It looks like a boy's handwriting because the letters are all sloppy. She reads it. She is touched by what he wrote.

"This kid has it rough," she says. "I feel for him. I remember when my grandmother had cancer. He really needs a friend."

"V. Morello, V. Morello, I don't know any V. Morello," Sally says. "I have to find him." She runs downstairs to find a phone book, scrambling for all the V. Morellos she can find.

When she finds the page for Morellos, she sees seven listings for "V. Morello." One by one, she calls each number.

"Excuse me,
do you know any
V. Morellos who are
getting chemo?"
she asks.

The first person who answers has a scratchy voice. He says, "Victor Morello speaking. Sorry, no cancer here."

The second person does not answer but there is an answering machine. It says, "Hello this is Vinny, happy as can be. Leave me a message. Will I call? We'll see."

He doesn't seem like he has cancer, Sally thinks.

The third person says, "Hola. ¿Cómo estás? Me llamo Vanessa."

Sally says, "Uhhhhhhhhhhhhhhhhh. Gracias." She doesn't understand a word and hangs up. The letter wasn't in Spanish, so this can't be her V. Morello.

She makes three more calls to Vance, Vaughn, and Violet, and none of them are going through chemo.

Only one more name left. Sally vows to herself that if this last call isn't the right V. Morello then she will stop trying.

On the seventh phone call a woman answers. Sally takes a deep breath. She asks, "Are there any V. Morellos getting chemo in this house?"

A startled voice says, "How do you know about my son Vincent?"

Sally jumps up. She starts doing the Dougie.

"You're the one I'm looking for! I got a message from your son. I want to do something special for him," Sally says.

"You got a message?" the mother asks. "What does the message say?"

"It says, 'I just want to feel like a kid again and play outside.'"

The phone goes very quiet.

"Hello?" Sally asks.

"I'm still here." Vincent's mother's voice cracks and she sniffles. "What do you have in mind?"

After an hour-long conversation with Vincent's mother Sally has formed a plan.

She goes to talk to her own mother who is a reporter for Channel Thirteen News.

Sally shows her mom the airplane and tells her about what she has gone through to find Vincent.

"You mean that airplane traveled all the way from REACH Children's Hospital to our house?" her mother asks. "That's a great story! We need to cover it."

As all of this is going on, Vincent is still lying in his hospital bed. There are paper airplanes scattered all around the floor.

The TV is on. The Wizards are supposed to play the Spurs later that day so he changes the channel to Channel Thirteen.

"BREAKING NEWS!" the screen says. It shows a reporter standing in front of a big building with a sign that says "REACH Children's Hospital."

"That's my hospital!" Vincent says, sitting up with total surprise.

The reporter is holding up a paper airplane and talking to a little girl. Vincent's mom is standing in the background.

"Wait! That's my mom! Is that my airplane, too?"

Then the reporter unfolds the airplane and reveals a message written there. She reads the words—his words—aloud.

Vincent can't believe it. He's thinking, *How and where did they find my airplane?*

The TV breaks to commercial, and the next thing Vincent knows, he hears lots of heavy footsteps in the hallway.

Then his mom opens his door, and a camera crew, the reporter, and the little girl follow behind her.

The lady starts to interview Vincent and she asks him, "What can we do to help?"

Vincent doesn't know what to say. He is feeling better lately and his doctor says he can get out of bed, but he can't go home yet.

He's tired of the hospital.
He's tired of the TV.
He's tired of cancer, tired of chemotherapy, and tired of being alone.

But what can these people do?

The reporter smiles and says, "Will a playground do?"

Vincent cries, "Yes! A playground would be more than enough!"

His mother says, "Wait. You still can't go outside yet. "

Then Sally says, "Well since he can't go outside, what about an indoor playroom? We can bring the fun to you."

Vincent's reaction is priceless. He is so excited that he starts to do the Cat Daddy.

Sally starts to laugh and says, "Wow, you're really good. Can you teach me before I leave?"

"Sure. By the way, thank you for finding my airplane."

"You can thank me by showing me how to do that dance!"

A week later, Sally knocks on his door.

For the past few days, Vincent has noticed people coming in and out of the hospital carrying tools and toys and paint and boxes.

He can't wait for the playroom to be finished.

"Sally, what's going on?"

"Well, come downstairs to the second floor and see what we've been working on."

Sally leads him downstairs to the old medical supply room. She opens the door.

Vincent is stunned.

Inside, a crowd of people yells:

SURPRISE!!

The room is bright with orange walls and the ceiling is painted blue with clouds. There are paper airplanes hanging down everywhere. It looks like an indoor playground, like Chuck E. Cheese, with airplanes painted all around the walls of the room. There's a balcony outside and a pile of kites to fly.

Vincent is overwhelmed with joy. "It's perfect. Now I can be a kid again."

"Does that mean you're ready to teach me that dance?"

Vincent starts to sing the song:

"Call me SpongeBob, stacking Krabby Patties, I go to work and do my Cat Daddy..."

Vincent and Sally do the Dougie and the Cat Daddy all the way around the playroom.

Wanna join them?

Acknowledgments

In July 2013, fifteen students embarked on an exciting journey. Tasked with creating original children's books, these young people brainstormed ideas, generated potential plots, wrote, revised, and provided critiques. In the end, four amazing books were created, showing again what teenagers can do when their potential is unleashed with purpose. Our fifteen authors have our immense gratitude and respect: Joshua, Jordan, Rashaan, Za'Metria, Marc, Sasha, Dana, Rico, Sejal, Angelo, Sean, Brandon, DaQuan, Kyare, and Zorita.

We also appreciate the leadership provided by our instructional leaders: Kaitlyn Denzler, Andrea Mirviss, and Brian Ovalles. Jusna Perrin, in addition to leading a team of teen writers, steered our summer program ship, seemingly with ease.

We also owe great thanks to our talented illustrators, Lucia Liu and Mira Ko, whose beautiful drawings brought these stories to life. And, most of all, we thank our dedicated and inspiring writing coach, Kathy Crutcher, who led our teens from the excitement of brainstorming through the hard work of revision to make these stories the best they can be.

Once the books were finished, publication costs could have made it difficult to share these stories with the world, so we appreciate the financial support provided by the New York Avenue Presbyterian Church, the Carr Family, the Denzler Family, Helen Runnells DuBois, the Hollowell Family, the Mirviss Family, and Cheryl Zabinski.

Most of all, we thank those of you who have purchased the books. We hope the smiles created as you read match those expressed as we wrote.

About the Authors

Marc Gaskins is from Washington, DC. He enjoys almost all sports and sees himself as a strong leader. He loves to cook and to play with animals. He also loves to spend money and to help the homeless.

Sasha Johnson is 16 years old and was born on August 16, 1996 in Baltimore, MD. She moved to Washington, DC at age 4 and has attended three different schools: Aton Elementary, Brookland Public Charter, and Hyde / Perry Street Prep. She is very talented!

About the Authors

Angelo Porter lives in Washington, DC. He is a 90s baby. He likes to play sports, and his favorite sport is rugby. When he grows up, Angelo would like to be an architect.

Sean Ross is 15 years old and a DC native. He enjoys playing sports, being with family and friends, sleeping, and eating. This is the first book that he has helped to write and hopefully not his last.

About the Illustrator

Mira Ko is a student at VCUarts. Someday she would love to work behind the scenes at an animation company or as a children's book illustrator. She loves to shoot photos, go on adventures, skate, and spend time with loved ones. More of her work can be found at mirako.carbonmade.com.

About the Story Coach

Kathy Crutcher has mentored young writers since 2003 and is passionate about empowering others to tell their stories. After coaching the teen tutors of Reach Incorporated to write their first four books in 2013, she was inspired to found Shout Mouse Press, a writing program and publishing house for unheard voices. To learn more, visit www.shoutmousepress.org.

About Reach Incorporated

Reach Incorporated develops confident grade-level readers and capable leaders by training teens to teach, creating academic benefit for all involved.

Founded in 2009, Reach recruits entering 9th grade students to be elementary school tutors. Elementary school students average 1.5 grade levels of reading growth per year of participation. This growth — equal to that created by highly effective teachers — is created by high school students who average more than two grade levels of growth per year of program participation.

Reach creates readers. Reach creates leaders. And, by lifting two populations through a uniquely structured relationship, Reach is effectively attacking Washington DC's literacy crisis.

During the summer of 2013, Reach launched a new program to build on school-year gains made by program tutors. As part of this program, teens partnered with professional writers and illustrators to create original children's stories. These stories, written entirely by our teens, provide our young people with the opportunity to share their talents and creativity with a wider audience.

By purchasing our books, you support student-led, community-driven efforts to improve educational outcomes in the District of Columbia.

Learn more at www.reachincorporated.org.

CPSIA information can be obtained at www.ICGtesting.com
Printed in the USA
BVOW07s0812260116

434212BV00002B/15/P